A PAIL OF AIR

A PAIL OF AIR

by Fritz Leiber

The dark star passed, bringing with it eternal night and turning history into incredible myth in a single generation!

*

Pa had sent me out to get an extra pail of air. I'd just about scooped it full and most of the warmth had leaked from my fingers when I saw the thing.

You know, at first I thought it was a young lady. Yes, a beautiful young lady's face all glowing in the dark and looking at me from the fifth floor of the opposite apartment, which hereabouts is the floor just above the white blanket of frozen air. I'd never seen a live young lady before, except in the old magazines—Sis is just a kid and Ma is pretty sick and miserable—and it gave me such a start that I dropped the pail. Who wouldn't, knowing everyone on Earth was dead except Pa and Ma and Sis and you?

Even at that, I don't suppose I should have been surprised. We all see things now and then. Ma has some pretty bad ones, to judge from the way she bugs her eyes at nothing and just screams and screams and huddles back against the blankets hanging around the Nest. Pa says it is natural we should react like that sometimes.

When I'd recovered the pail and could look again at the opposite apartment, I got an idea of what Ma might be feeling at those times, for I saw it wasn't a young lady at all but simply a light—a tiny light that moved stealthily from window to window, just as if one of the cruel little stars had come down out of the airless sky to investigate why the Earth had gone away from the Sun, and maybe to hunt down something to torment or terrify, now that the Earth didn't have the Sun's protection.

I tell you, the thought of it gave me the creeps. I just stood there shaking, and almost froze my feet and did frost my helmet so solid on the inside that I couldn't have seen the light even if

4

it had come out of one of the windows to get me. Then I had the wit to go back inside.

Pretty soon I was feeling my familiar way through the thirty or so blankets and rugs Pa has got hung around to slow down the escape of air from the Nest, and I wasn't quite so scared. I began to hear the tick-ticking of the clocks in the Nest and knew I was getting back into air, because there's no sound outside in the vacuum, of course. But my mind was still crawly and uneasy as I pushed through the last blankets—Pa's got them faced with aluminum foil to hold in the heat—and came into the Nest.

*

Let me tell you about the Nest. It's low and snug, just room for the four of us and our things. The floor is covered with thick woolly rugs. Three of the sides are blankets, and the blankets roofing it touch Pa's head. He tells me it's inside a much bigger room, but I've never seen the real walls or ceiling.

Against one of the blanket-walls is a big set of shelves, with tools and books and other stuff, and on top of it a whole row of clocks. Pa's very fussy about keeping them wound. He says we must never forget time, and without a sun or moon, that would be easy to do.

The fourth wall has blankets all over except around the fireplace, in which there is a fire that must never go out. It keeps us from freezing and does a lot more besides. One of us must always watch it. Some of the clocks are alarm and we can use them to remind us. In the early days there was only Ma to take turns with Pa—I think of that when she gets difficult—but now there's me to help, and Sis too.

It's Pa who is the chief guardian of the fire, though. I always think of him that way: a tall man sitting cross-legged, frowning anxiously at the fire, his lined face golden in its light, and every so often carefully placing on it a piece of coal from the big heap beside it. Pa tells me there used to be guardians of the fire sometimes in the very old days—vestal virgins, he calls them—although there was unfrozen air all around then and you didn't really need one.

He was sitting just that way now, though he got up quick to take the pail from me and bawl me out for loitering—he'd spotted my frozen helmet right off. That roused Ma and she joined in picking on me. She's always trying to get the load off her feelings, Pa explains. He shut her up pretty fast. Sis let off a couple of silly squeals too.

Pa handled the pail of air in a twist of cloth. Now that it was inside the Nest, you could really feel its coldness. It just seemed to suck the heat out of everything. Even the flames cringed away from it as Pa put it down close by the fire.

Yet it's that glimmery white stuff in the pail that keeps us alive. It slowly melts and vanishes and refreshes the Nest and feeds the fire. The blankets keep it from escaping too fast. Pa'd like to seal the whole place, but he can't—building's too earthquake-twisted, and besides he has to leave the chimney open for smoke.

Pa says air is tiny molecules that fly away like a flash if there isn't something to stop them. We have to watch sharp not to let the air run low. Pa always keeps a big reserve supply of it in buckets behind the first blankets, along with extra coal and cans of food and other things, such as pails of snow to melt for water. We have to go way down to the bottom floor for that stuff, which is a mean trip, and get it through a door to outside.

You see, when the Earth got cold, all the water in the air froze first and made a blanket ten feet thick or so everywhere, and then down on top of that dropped the crystals of frozen air, making another white blanket sixty or seventy feet thick maybe.

Of course, all the parts of the air didn't freeze and snow down at the same time.

First to drop out was the carbon dioxide—when you're

shoveling for water, you have to make sure you don't go too high and get any of that stuff mixed in, for it would put you to sleep, maybe for good, and make the fire go out. Next there's the nitrogen, which doesn't count one way or the other, though it's the biggest part of the blanket. On top of that and easy to get at, which is lucky for us, there's the oxygen that keeps us alive. Pa says we live better than kings ever did, breathing pure oxygen, but we're used to it and don't notice. Finally, at the very top, there's a slick of liquid helium, which is funny stuff. All of these gases in neat separate layers. Like a pussy caffay, Pa laughingly says, whatever that is.

*

I was busting to tell them all about what I'd seen, and so as soon as I'd ducked out of my helmet and while I was still climbing out of my suit, I cut loose. Right away Ma got nervous and began making eyes at the entry-slit in the blankets and wringing her hands together—the hand where she'd lost three fingers from frostbite inside the good one, as usual. I could tell that Pa was annoyed at me scaring her and wanted to explain it all away quickly, yet could see I wasn't fooling.

"And you watched this light for some time, son?" he asked when I finished.

I hadn't said anything about first thinking it was a young lady's face. Somehow that part embarrassed me.

"Long enough for it to pass five windows and go to the next floor."

"And it didn't look like stray electricity or crawling liquid or starlight focused by a growing crystal, or anything like that?"

He wasn't just making up those ideas. Odd things happen in a world that's about as cold as can be, and just when you think matter would be frozen dead, it takes on a strange new life. A slimy stuff comes crawling toward the Nest, just like an animal snuffing for heat—that's the liquid helium. And once, when I was little, a bolt of lightning—not even Pa could figure where it came from—hit the nearby steeple and crawled up and down it for weeks, until the glow finally died.

"Not like anything I ever saw," I told him.

He stood for a moment frowning. Then, "I'll go out with you, and you show it to me," he said.

Ma raised a howl at the idea of being left alone, and Sis joined in, too, but Pa quieted them. We started climbing into our outside clothes—mine had been warming by the fire. Pa made them. They have plastic headpieces that were once big double-duty transparent food cans, but they keep heat and air in and can replace the air for a little while, long enough for our trips for water and coal and food and so on.

Ma started moaning again, "I've always known there was something outside there, waiting to get us. I've felt it for years—something that's part of the cold and hates all warmth and wants to destroy the Nest. It's been watching us all this time, and now it's coming after us. It'll get you and then come for me. Don't go, Harry!"

Pa had everything on but his helmet. He knelt by the fireplace and reached in and shook the long metal rod that goes up the chimney and knocks off the ice that keeps trying to clog it. Once a week he goes up on the roof to check if it's working all right. That's our worst trip and Pa won't let me make it alone.

"Sis," Pa said quietly, "come watch the fire. Keep an eye on the air, too. If it gets low or doesn't seem to be boiling fast enough, fetch another bucket from behind the blanket. But mind your hands. Use the cloth to pick up the bucket."

Sis quit helping Ma be frightened and came over and did as she was told. Ma quieted down pretty suddenly, though her eyes were still kind of wild as she watched Pa fix on his helmet tight and pick up a pail and the two of us go out.

*

8

Pa led the way and I took hold of his belt. It's a funny thing, I'm not afraid to go by myself, but when Pa's along I always want to hold on to him. Habit, I guess, and then there's no denying that this time I was a bit scared.

You see, it's this way. We know that everything is dead out there. Pa heard the last radio voices fade away years ago, and had seen some of the last folks die who weren't as lucky or well-protected as us. So we knew that if there was something groping around out there, it couldn't be anything human or friendly.

Besides that, there's a feeling that comes with it always being night, *cold* night. Pa says there used to be some of that feeling even in the old days, but then every morning the Sun would come and chase it away. I have to take his word for that, not ever remembering the Sun as being anything more than a big star. You see, I hadn't been born when the dark star snatched us away from the Sun, and by now it's dragged us out beyond the orbit of the planet Pluto, Pa says, and taking us farther out all the time.

I found myself wondering whether there mightn't be something on the dark star that wanted us, and if that was why it had captured the Earth. Just then we came to the end of the corridor and I followed Pa out on the balcony.

I don't know what the city looked like in the old days, but now it's beautiful. The starlight lets you see it pretty well—there's quite a bit of light in those steady points speckling the blackness above. (Pa says the stars used to twinkle once, but that was because there was air.) We are on a hill and the shimmery plain drops away from us and then flattens out, cut up into neat squares by the troughs that used to be streets. I sometimes make my mashed potatoes look like it, before I pour on the gravy.

Some taller buildings push up out of the feathery plain, topped by rounded caps of air crystals, like the fur hood Ma wears, only whiter. On those buildings you can see the darker squares of windows, underlined by white dashes of air crystals. Some of them are on a slant, for many of the buildings are pretty badly twisted by the quakes and all the rest that happened when the dark star captured the Earth.

Here and there a few icicles hang, water icicles from the first days of the cold, other icicles of frozen air that melted on the roofs and dripped and froze again. Sometimes one of those icicles will catch the light of a star and send it to you so brightly you think the star has swooped into the city. That was one of the things Pa had been thinking of when I told him about the light, but I had thought of it myself first and known it wasn't so.

He touched his helmet to mine so we could talk easier and he asked me to point out the windows to him. But there wasn't any light moving around inside them now, or anywhere else. To my surprise, Pa didn't bawl me out and tell me I'd been seeing things. He looked all around quite a while after filling his pail, and just as we were going inside he whipped around without warning, as if to take some peeping thing off guard.

I could feel it, too. The old peace was gone. There was something lurking out there, watching, waiting, getting ready.

Inside, he said to me, touching helmets, "If you see something like that again, son, don't tell the others. Your Ma's sort of nervous these days and we owe her all the feeling of safety we can give her. Once—it was when your sister was born—I was ready to give up and die, but your Mother kept me trying. Another time she kept the fire going a whole week all by herself when I was sick. Nursed me and took care of the two of you, too."

*

"You know that game we sometimes play, sitting in a square in the Nest, tossing a ball around? Courage is like a ball, son. A person can hold it only so long, and then he's got to toss it to someone else. When it's tossed your way, you've got to catch it and hold it tight—and hope there'll be someone else to toss it to when you get tired of being brave."

His talking to me that way made me feel grown-up and good. But it didn't wipe away the thing outside from the back of my mind—or the fact that Pa took it seriously.

*

It's hard to hide your feelings about such a thing. When we got back in the Nest and took off our outside clothes, Pa laughed about it all and told them it was nothing and kidded me for having such an imagination, but his words fell flat. He didn't convince Ma and Sis any more than he did me. It looked for a minute like we were all fumbling the courage-ball. Something had to be done, and almost before I knew what I was going to say, I heard myself asking Pa to tell us about the old days, and how it all happened.

He sometimes doesn't mind telling that story, and Sis and I sure like to listen to it, and he got my idea. So we were all settled around the fire in a wink, and Ma pushed up some cans to thaw for supper, and Pa began. Before he did, though, I noticed him casually get a hammer from the shelf and lay it down beside him.

It was the same old story as always—I think I could recite the main thread of it in my sleep—though Pa always puts in a new detail or two and keeps improving it in spots.

He told us how the Earth had been swinging around the Sun ever so steady and warm, and the people on it fixing to make money and wars and have a good time and get power and treat each other right or wrong, when without warning there comes charging out of space this dead star, this burned out sun, and upsets everything.

You know, I find it hard to believe in the way those people felt, any more than I can believe in the swarming number of them. Imagine people getting ready for the horrible sort of war they were cooking up. Wanting it even, or at least wishing it were over so as to end their nervousness. As if all folks didn't have to hang together and pool every bit of warmth just to keep alive. And how can they have hoped to end danger, any more than we can hope to end the cold?

Sometimes I think Pa exaggerates and makes things out too black. He's cross with us once in a while and was probably cross with all those folks. Still, some of the things I read in the old magazines sound pretty wild. He may be right.

*

The dark star, as Pa went on telling it, rushed in pretty fast and there wasn't much time to get ready. At the beginning they tried to keep it a secret from most people, but then the truth came out, what with the earthquakes and floods—imagine, oceans of *unfrozen* water!—and people seeing stars blotted out by something on a clear night. First off they thought it would hit the Sun, and then they thought it would hit the Earth. There was even the start of a rush to get to a place called China, because people thought the star would hit on the other side. But then they found it wasn't going to hit either side, but was going to come very close to the Earth.

Most of the other planets were on the other side of the Sun and didn't get involved. The Sun and the newcomer fought over the Earth for a little while—pulling it this way and that, like two dogs growling over a bone, Pa described it this time—and then the newcomer won and carried us off. The Sun got a consolation prize, though. At the last minute he managed to hold on to the Moon.

That was the time of the monster earthquakes and floods, twenty times worse than anything before. It was also the time of the Big Jerk, as Pa calls it, when all Earth got yanked suddenly, just as Pa has done to me once or twice, grabbing me by the collar to do it, when I've been sitting too far from the fire.

You see, the dark star was going through space faster than the Sun, and in the opposite direction, and it had to wrench the world considerably in order to take it away.

The Big Jerk didn't last long. It was over as soon as the Earth was settled down in its new orbit around the dark star. But it was pretty terrible while it lasted. Pa says that all sorts of cliffs and buildings toppled, oceans slopped over, swamps and sandy deserts gave great sliding surges that buried nearby lands. Earth was almost jerked out of its atmosphere blanket and the air got so thin in spots that people keeled over and fainted—though of course, at the same time, they were getting knocked down by the Big Jerk and maybe their bones broke or skulls cracked.

We've often asked Pa how people acted during that time, whether they were scared or brave or crazy or stunned, or all four, but he's sort of leery of the subject, and he was again tonight. He says he was mostly too busy to notice.

You see, Pa and some scientist friends of his had figured out part of what was going to happen—they'd known we'd get captured and our air would freeze—and they'd been working like mad to fix up a place with airtight walls and doors, and insulation against the cold, and big supplies of food and fuel and water and bottled air. But the place got smashed in the last earthquakes and all Pa's friends were killed then and in the Big Jerk. So he had to start over and throw the Nest together quick without any advantages, just using any stuff he could lay his hands on.

I guess he's telling pretty much the truth when he says he didn't have any time to keep an eye on how other folks behaved, either then or in the Big Freeze that followed—followed very quick, you know, both because the dark star was pulling us away very fast and because Earth's rotation had been slowed in the tug-of-war, so that the nights were ten old nights long.

Still, I've got an idea of some of the things that happened from the frozen folk I've seen, a few of them in other rooms in our building, others clustered around the furnaces in the basements where we go for coal.

In one of the rooms, an old man sits stiff in a chair, with an arm and a leg in splints. In another, a man and woman are huddled together in a bed with heaps of covers over them. You can just see their heads peeking out, close together. And in another a beautiful young lady is sitting with a pile of wraps huddled around her, looking hopefully toward the door, as if waiting for someone who never came back with warmth and food. They're all still and stiff as statues, of course, but just like life.

Pa showed them to me once in quick winks of his flashlight, when he still had a fair supply of batteries and could afford to waste a little light. They scared me pretty bad and made my heart pound, especially the young lady.

*

Now, with Pa telling his story for the umpteenth time to take our minds off another scare, I got to thinking of the frozen folk again. All of a sudden I got an idea that scared me worse than anything yet. You see, I'd just remembered the face I'd thought I'd seen in the window. I'd forgotten about that on account of trying to hide it from the others.

What, I asked myself, if the frozen folk were coming to life? What if they were like the liquid helium that got a new lease on life and started crawling toward the heat just when you thought its molecules ought to freeze solid forever? Or like the electricity that moves endlessly when it's just about as cold as that? What if the ever-growing cold, with the temperature creeping down the last few degrees to the last zero, had mysteriously wakened the frozen folk to life—not warm-blooded life, but something icy and horrible?

That was a worse idea than the one about something coming down from the dark star to get us.

Or maybe, I thought, both ideas might be true. Something coming down from the dark star and making the frozen folk move, using them to do its work. That would fit with both things I'd seen—the beautiful young lady and the moving, starlike light.

The frozen folk with minds from the dark star behind their unwinking eyes, creeping, crawling, snuffing their way, following the heat to the Nest.

I tell you, that thought gave me a very bad turn and I wanted very badly to tell the others my fears, but I remembered what Pa had said and clenched my teeth and didn't speak.

We were all sitting very still. Even the fire was burning silently. There was just the sound of Pa's voice and the clocks.

And then, from beyond the blankets, I thought I heard a tiny noise. My skin tightened all over me.

Pa was telling about the early years in the Nest and had come to the place where he philosophizes.

"So I asked myself then," he said, "what's the use of going on? What's the use of dragging it out for a few years? Why prolong a doomed existence of hard work and cold and loneliness? The human race is done. The Earth is done. Why not give up, I asked myself—and all of a sudden I got the answer."

Again I heard the noise, louder this time, a kind of uncertain, shuffling tread, coming closer. I couldn't breathe.

"Life's always been a business of working hard and fighting the cold," Pa was saying. "The earth's always been a lonely place, millions of miles from the next planet. And no matter how long the human race might have lived, the end would have come some night. Those things don't matter. What matters is that life is good. It has a lovely texture, like some rich cloth or fur, or the petals of flowers—you've seen pictures of those, but I can't describe how they feel—or the fire's glow. It makes everything else worth while. And that's as true for the last man as the first."

And still the steps kept shuffling closer. It seemed to me that the inmost blanket trembled and bulged a little. Just as if they were burned into my imagination, I kept seeing those peering, frozen eyes.

"So right then and there," Pa went on, and now I could tell that he heard the steps, too, and was talking loud so we maybe wouldn't hear them, "right then and there I told myself that I was going on as if we had all eternity ahead of us. I'd have children and teach them all I could. I'd get them to read books. I'd plan for the future, try to enlarge and seal the Nest. I'd do what I could to keep everything beautiful and growing. I'd keep alive my feeling of wonder even at the cold and the dark and the distant stars."

But then the blanket actually did move and lift. And there was a bright light somewhere behind it. Pa's voice stopped and his eyes turned to the widening slit and his hand went out until it touched and gripped the handle of the hammer beside him.

*

In through the blanket stepped the beautiful young lady. She stood there looking at us the strangest way, and she carried something bright and unwinking in her hand. And two other faces peered over her shoulders—men's faces, white and staring.

Well, my heart couldn't have been stopped for more than four or five beats before I realized she was wearing a suit and helmet like Pa's homemade ones, only fancier, and that the men were, too—and that the frozen folk certainly wouldn't be wearing those. Also, I noticed that the bright thing in her hand was just a kind of flashlight.

The silence kept on while I swallowed hard a couple of times, and after that there was all sorts of jabbering and commotion.

They were simply people, you see. We hadn't been the only ones to survive; we'd just thought so, for natural enough reasons. These three people had survived, and quite a few others with them. And when we found out *how* they'd survived, Pa let out the biggest whoop of joy.

They were from Los Alamos and they were getting their heat and power from atomic energy. Just using the uranium and plutonium intended for bombs, they had enough to go on for thousands of years. They had a regular little airtight city, with air-locks and all. They even generated electric light and grew plants and animals by it. (At this Pa let out a second whoop, waking Ma from her faint.)

But if we were flabbergasted at them, they were double-flabbergasted at us.

One of the men kept saying, "But it's impossible, I tell you. You can't maintain an air supply without hermetic sealing. It's simply impossible."

That was after he had got his helmet off and was using our air. Meanwhile, the young lady kept looking around at us as if we were saints, and telling us we'd done something amazing, and suddenly she broke down and cried.

They'd been scouting around for survivors, but they never expected to find any in a place like this. They had rocket ships at Los Alamos and plenty of chemical fuel. As for liquid oxygen, all you had to do was go out and shovel the air blanket at the top *level*. So after they'd got things going smoothly at Los Alamos, which had taken years, they'd decided to make some trips to likely places where there might be other survivors. No good trying long-distance radio signals, of course, since there was no atmosphere to carry them around the curve of the Earth.

Well, they'd found other colonies at Argonne and Brookhaven and way around the world at Harwell and Tanna

Tuva. And now they'd been giving our city a look, not really expecting to find anything. But they had an instrument that noticed the faintest heat waves and it had told them there was something warm down here, so they'd landed to investigate. Of course we hadn't heard them land, since there was no air to carry the sound, and they'd had to investigate around quite a while before finding us. Their instruments had given them a wrong steer and they'd wasted some time in the building across the street.

*

By now, all five adults were talking like sixty. Pa was demonstrating to the men how he worked the fire and got rid of the ice in the chimney and all that. Ma had perked up wonderfully and was showing the young lady her cooking and sewing stuff, and even asking about how the women dressed at Los Alamos. The strangers marveled at everything and praised it to the skies. I could tell from the way they wrinkled their noses that they found the Nest a bit smelly, but they never mentioned that at all and just asked bushels of questions.

In fact, there was so much talking and excitement that Pa forgot about things, and it wasn't until they were all getting groggy that he looked and found the air had all boiled away in the pail. He got another bucket of air quick from behind the blankets. Of course that started them all laughing and jabbering again. The newcomers even got a little drunk. They weren't used to so much oxygen.

Funny thing, though—I didn't do much talking at all and Sis hung on to Ma all the time and hid her face when anybody looked at her. I felt pretty uncomfortable and disturbed myself, even about the young lady. Glimpsing her outside there, I'd had all sorts of mushy thoughts, but now I was just embarrassed and scared of her, even though she tried to be nice as anything to me.

I sort of wished they'd all quit crowding the Nest and let us be alone and get our feelings straightened out.

And when the newcomers began to talk about our all going to Los Alamos, as if that were taken for granted, I could see that something of the same feeling struck Pa and Ma, too. Pa got very silent all of a sudden and Ma kept telling the young lady, "But I wouldn't know how to act there and I haven't any clothes."

The strangers were puzzled like anything at first, but then they got the idea. As Pa kept saying, "It just doesn't seem right to let this fire go out."

*

Well, the strangers are gone, but they're coming back. It hasn't been decided yet just what will happen. Maybe the Nest will be kept up as what one of the strangers called a "survival school." Or maybe we will join the pioneers who are going to try to establish a new colony at the uranium mines at Great Slave Lake or in the Congo.

Of course, now that the strangers are gone, I've been thinking a lot about Los Alamos and those other tremendous colonies. I have a hankering to see them for myself.

You ask me, Pa wants to see them, too. He's been getting pretty thoughtful, watching Ma and Sis perk up.

"It's different, now that we know others are alive," he explains to me. "Your mother doesn't feel so hopeless any more. Neither do I, for that matter, not having to carry the whole responsibility for keeping the human race going, so to speak. It scares a person."

I looked around at the blanket walls and the fire and the pails of air boiling away and Ma and Sis sleeping in the warmth and the flickering light.

"It's not going to be easy to leave the Nest," I said, wanting to cry, kind of. "It's so small and there's just the four of us. I get scared at the idea of big places and a lot of strangers."

He nodded and put another piece of coal on the fire. Then he looked at the little pile and grinned suddenly and put a couple of handfuls on, just as if it was one of our birthdays or Christmas.

"You'll quickly get over that feeling son," he said. "The trouble with the world was that it kept getting smaller and smaller, till it ended with just the Nest. Now it'll be good to have a real huge world again, the way it was in the beginning."

I guess he's right. You think the beautiful young lady will wait for me till I grow up? I'll be twenty in only ten years.

www.ingramcontent.com/pod-product-compliance
Lightning Source LLC
Chambersburg PA
CBHW020144150626
46552CB00021B/1701